Dear Parents and Educators,

Welcome to Penguin Young Readers! As parents and educators, you know that each child develops at his or her own pace—in terms of speech, critical thinking, and, of course, reading. Penguin Young Readers recognizes this fact. As a result, each Penguin Young Readers book is assigned a traditional easy-to-read level (1–4) as well as a Guided Reading Level (A–P). Both of these systems will help you choose the right book for your child. Please refer to the back of each book for specific leveling information. Penguin Young Readers features esteemed authors and illustrators, stories about favorite characters, fascinating nonfiction, and more!

Fox All Week

LEVEL **3**

GUIDED READING LEVEL **J**

This book is perfect for a **Transitional Reader** who:
* can read multisyllable and compound words;
* can read words with prefixes and suffixes;
* is able to identify story elements (beginning, middle, end, plot, setting, characters, problem, solution); and
* can understand different points of view.

Here are some **activities** you can do during and after reading this book:
* Chapter Titles: The title of each chapter is very important. It should catch the reader's attention and say something about the chapter. Each of the seven chapters in this book has a title based on the time and/or setting. Work with the child to come up with a new title for each chapter based on what happens in the chapter.
* Idioms: An idiom is a word or group of words that has a special meaning when read all together. Reread the following idioms with the child, and discuss their meanings: "raining cats and dogs" (page 8), "poor thing" (page 11), "laughing herself silly" (page 24), "as sick as dogs" (page 28), "hopping mad" (page 29), "gave Fox a look" (page 40), and "until the bugs came out" (page 48).

Remember, sharing the love of reading with a child is the best gift you can give!

—Bonnie Bader, EdM
　Penguin Young Readers program

W9-BXL-834

*Penguin Young Readers are leveled by independent reviewers applying the standards developed by Irene Fountas and Gay Su Pinnell in *Matching Books to Readers: Using Leveled Books in Guided Reading*, Heinemann, 1999.

For Judith Blum

Penguin Young Readers
Published by the Penguin Group
Penguin Group (USA) Inc., 375 Hudson Street, New York, New York 10014, USA
Penguin Group (Canada), 90 Eglinton Avenue East, Suite 700, Toronto, Ontario M4P 2Y3, Canada
(a division of Pearson Penguin Canada Inc.)
Penguin Books Ltd, 80 Strand, London WC2R 0RL, England
Penguin Ireland, 25 St Stephen's Green, Dublin 2, Ireland (a division of Penguin Books Ltd)
Penguin Group (Australia), 707 Collins Street, Melbourne, Victoria 3008, Australia
(a division of Pearson Australia Group Pty Ltd)
Penguin Books India Pvt Ltd, 11 Community Centre, Panchsheel Park, New Delhi—110 017, India
Penguin Group (NZ), 67 Apollo Drive, Rosedale, Auckland 0632, New Zealand
(a division of Pearson New Zealand Ltd)
Penguin Books (South Africa), Rosebank Office Park, 181 Jan Smuts Avenue,
Parktown North 2193, South Africa
Penguin China, B7 Jiaming Center, 27 East Third Ring Road North,
Chaoyang District, Beijing 100020, China

Penguin Books Ltd, Registered Offices: 80 Strand, London WC2R 0RL, England

Text copyright © 1984 by Edward Marshall. Pictures copyright © 1984 by James Marshall.
All rights reserved. First published in 1984 by Dial Books for Young Readers, an imprint of
Penguin Group (USA) Inc. Published in a Puffin Easy-to-Read edition in 1995. Published in 2013
by Penguin Young Readers, an imprint of Penguin Group (USA) Inc., 345 Hudson Street,
New York, New York 10014. Manufactured in China.

The Library of Congress has catalogued the Dial edition
under the following Control Number: 84001708

ISBN 978-0-14-037708-8   10 9 8 7 6 5 4

PENGUIN YOUNG READERS

LEVEL
3
TRANSITIONAL
READER

FOX ALL WEEK

by Edward Marshall
pictures by James Marshall

Penguin Young Readers
An Imprint of Penguin Group (USA) Inc.

MONDAY MORNING

On Monday morning

Fox was up in a flash.

"Hot dog!" he cried.

"Today Miss Moon's class

is going on a big field trip!

We'll have lots of fun!"

But when Fox looked outside,

he could not believe his eyes.

It was raining cats and dogs.

"Rats!" said Fox.

"This isn't funny."

The rain came down harder.

"School won't be any fun today,"
said Fox.

At breakfast Fox was very quiet.

"I have a sore throat," he said.

"But I will go to school, anyway."

"Oh no," said Mom.

"You will go straight to bed."

"If you say so," said Fox.

Fox got all nice and cozy.

He read his comic books.

He listened to the radio.

And he got lots of attention.

Outside it was still raining.

"I did the right thing," said Fox.

"Feeling any better?"
said Mom.

"Oh no," said Fox.

"I feel much worse."

"Poor thing," said Mom.

Just then Fox heard voices.

It was Miss Moon and the class.

"We are off on our field trip!"
called out Carmen.

"A little rain can't stop us!"
said Miss Moon.

"This isn't funny," said Fox.

TUESDAY'S LUNCH

Tuesday was sunny and hot.

"You may eat lunch outside,"

said Miss Moon.

"Let's go!" cried the class.

And they all went outside.

Fox, Carmen, and Dexter sat down and opened their lunches.

"Ugh!" said Carmen.

"Tuna fish!"

"Ugh, tuna fish!" said Fox.

"Oh no!" said Dexter.

"Tuna fish!"

"Let's throw our lunches away,"
said Fox.

"Let's do!" said the others.

They were so proud of themselves.

"This will teach Mom,"
said Dexter.

But soon they were very hungry.
"Whose idea was this, anyway?"
said Fox.

"Guess!" said his friends.
After school they ran to look
for their sandwiches.

On the other side of the wall

they met a poor old cat.

"I'm so happy," said the old cat.

"A nice lunch fell from the sky!"

"Three tuna sandwiches?" said Fox.

"Gosh," said the old cat.

"Kids are really smart these days."

WEDNESDAY EVENING AT THE LIBRARY

"I like books that make me cry,"
said Carmen.

"I like books that give me
the creeps," said Dexter.

"I like books that make me laugh,"
said Fox.

"This is the funniest book
I've ever read."

And he laughed out loud.

"Control yourself!" said Carmen.

"Here comes Miss Pencil!"

"Now see here, Fox!"
said Miss Pencil.

But Fox couldn't stop laughing.

"That does it!" said Miss Pencil.

"You will have to leave.

And take your friends with you!"

"Fox got us into trouble,"
said Dexter.

"I couldn't help it," said Fox.

Suddenly they heard laughing.

They peeked in the

library window.

It was Miss Pencil.

She was reading Fox's book

and laughing herself silly.

"She's rolling around on the floor,"

said Dexter.

"Miss Pencil is strange," said Carmen.

THURSDAY AFTER SCHOOL

On Thursday Dexter found
a box of cigars on the sidewalk.
"I smoke cigars all the time,"
said Fox.
"You *do?*" said his friends.

"Mom doesn't care," said Fox.

"She *doesn't?*" said his friends.

"Let's smoke now," said Fox.

"Why not?" said his friends.

And they went someplace quiet.

Soon they were as sick as dogs.

"I didn't know it would be
like *this*!" said Fox.

"What!" cried Carmen.

"You said you smoke all the time!"

"I told a fib," said Fox.

"Really, Fox!" said Carmen.

"That makes me hopping mad!"

"I won't do it again," said Fox.

In an hour they felt better.

But Dexter kept on smoking.

"It makes me look smart," he said.

"Really, Dexter!" said his friends.

THE
FRIDAY
DINNER

Fox's mom was not a good cook.

"Rats!" said Mom.

"I've done it again!"

"Never fear, Fox is here," said Fox.

"*I* will cook dinner."

"Oh goody!" said Mom.

"Uh-oh," said Louise.

"I must be left alone," said Fox.

"Come, Louise," said Mom.

Mom and Louise sat down.

They waited a long time.

They heard terrible noises.

CRASH! BANG! SMASH! SPLAT!

Finally dinner was ready.

"Fox," said Mom,

"these peanut butter and jelly

sandwiches are simply delicious."

THE
SATURDAY
VISIT

"Fox, dear!" called Mom.

"Maybe she won't see me,"
said Fox.

"Yoo-hoo! Fox!" called Mom.

"I won't make a sound," said Fox.

But suddenly he had to—

"AH-CHOO!"

"Ah-ha!" cried Mom.

"I was doing homework," said Fox.

"Hmmm," said Mom.

"You will have to do it later.
You and Louise must visit Grannie.
It's her birthday."

"Good old Grannie Fox," said Fox.

"Put on a white shirt and tie," said Mom.

"But it's Saturday!" cried Fox.

"You heard me," said Mom.

"I won't do it," said Fox.

But Mom got her way.

"There!" she said.

"You look very sweet

Now don't forget to give Grannie

these chocolates."

"Come on, Louise," said Fox.

On the way to Grannie's house
they met a pretty fox.
"What a cute tie,"
said the pretty fox.
"I always wear ties," said Fox.

Louise gave Fox a look.

"Chocolates!" cried the pretty fox.

"They are for you," said Fox.

"How sweet!" said the pretty fox.

And she took the chocolates.

"Bye-bye!" she said.

"What have I done?" said Fox.

At Grannie's house Fox told
the truth about the chocolates.
"That's okay," said Grannie.
"I'll make us some fudge instead.
Now take off that hot tie."

"Gosh," said Fox.
"Grannies are great!"

SUNDAY EVENING

"Look," said Dexter.

"That must be a new kid in town."

"Why does she have a paper bag over her head?" said Fox.

"Maybe she isn't very pretty," said Carmen.

"Maybe she's shy," said Dexter.

"It isn't easy being a new kid," said Fox.

"True," said the others.

"Hello there!" called out Fox.

The new kid stopped.

She turned around.

And just then a big wind

blew away the paper bag.

Fox couldn't believe his eyes.

It was his friend Raisin!

"I got braces," she said softly.

"Oh, let's see!" said Carmen.

And everybody had a good look.

"Very pretty," they said.

"I'm getting braces soon,"
said Fox.

"They don't hurt," said Raisin.

Soon they all got tired of
talking about braces.
"Want to play with us?" said Fox.
"Sure!" said Raisin.

And they all played
until the bugs came out.